TOBE

TOBE

By

Stella Gentry Sharpe

Photographs

by

Charles Farrell

Chapel Hill

The University of North Carolina Press

ACKNOWLEDGMENTS

I am especially indebted to Dr. M. R. Trabue, formerly head of the Department of Education in the University of North Carolina, now Dean of the School of Education in Pennsylvania State College, for encouragement in the writing of *Tobe;* to Miss Nora Beust, of the School of Library Science in the University of North Carolina; to Dr. Guy B. Johnson and Dr. L. M. Brooks, of the Department of Sociology in the University of North Carolina, for reading the manuscript and making many helpful suggestions; to Mrs. Alice T. Paine, of the University of North Carolina Press, for her editing of the manuscript; and to Mr. Charles Farrell, whose photographs have caught the spirit of the text so completely and have made possible the carrying out of a long delayed plan.

STELLA GENTRY SHARPE

CONTENTS

TOBE AND HIS BROTHERS

This is Tobe and his brothers.
They live on a farm.
They have many pets.
Tobe is not a big boy.
He has no twin.
Can you find him?

TOBE

I am Tobe.

My real name is Clay Junior.

Tobe is a nickname.

I am six years old.

I go to school.

We have fun on our farm.

I will tell you about it.

RAEFORD

Raeford is my big brother.
He is twelve years old.
In winter he goes to school.
In summer he helps Daddy work on the farm.
He does not like to work with a hoe.
He likes to feed the animals.

ALTON AND ALVIS

Alton and Alvis are twins.
They are nine years old.
In winter they go to school.
They can read, write, dance, and sing.
They like to dance together.
Alton has a nickname.
His nickname is Little Boy.
Alvis has a nickname.
His nickname is Big Boy.

WILLIAM AND RUFUS

William and Rufus are twins.
They are just five years old.
They do not go to school.
They do not have nicknames.
They love each other very much.
They help each other work.
They help each other fight, too.
They can whip me.
I do not have a twin to help me.

MOTHER AND DADDY

Here are Mother and Daddy.
On Sundays they go to church.
They do not go to school.
In winter they sit by the fire.
Mother sews and Daddy reads.
They listen to the radio.
Sometimes they sing and tell us stories.
In summer Daddy works on the farm,
   and Mother cans food for winter.

TOBE'S SISTERS

I have two big sisters.
They are not twins.
Lily Mae is thirteen, and Mary Lee is fourteen.
In winter they go to school.
In summer they help Mother.

They can wash, iron, cook, and sew.
They laugh and talk all the time.
I don't know what they talk about.
Maybe it is a secret.

TOM, OUR PET CAT

This is our pet cat. His name is Tom.
One day a big boy caught our cat
   and put him in the brook.
We called our Mother.
She made the big boy go home.

[14]

We feed our cat and play with him.
We do not hurt him.
He is not afraid of us.

OUR SCHOOL

This is our school.
We keep it nice and clean.
We have trees in the yard.
We are planting some bushes.
When they grow, the yard will be pretty.

OUR CHURCH

This is our church.
We take good care of it.
We like to go to church and sing and sing.
Sometimes we have good dinners under the trees.
We like that, too.

THE PET BABY CHICKS

William and Rufus have some pet baby chicks.
The chicks are very little.
An old dog killed their mother.
William and Rufus like to feed the pet baby chicks.
They feed the chicks bread.
They give them milk and water to drink.
Every day they let the chicks play in the sun.
At night they put them in a warm box.

OUR GOAT

This is our pet goat. Her name is Nannie.
We feed her bread and corn.
She likes green leaves, too.
Nannie is very strong. She likes to play.
She jumps very high. She can climb a short ladder.
William and Rufus are too little to play with Nannie,
  but they like to see her eat.
Our cousin, John Henry, likes to see her eat, too.

THE HENS

My Mother keeps hens.
I feed the hens corn and bread.
Sometimes I give them milk to drink.
The hens are tame.
They will eat from my hand.
The hens lay many eggs.
I like the eggs.
They make me strong.

THE PIGS

Daddy has two pigs. They are big pigs.
We like to feed the pigs.
We feed them corn and sweet potatoes.
Sometimes we feed them peanuts.
We can ride the pigs, but they do not make good horses.
  They will not go right.
Mother says we are too big to ride the pigs.

Daddy gave us five little pigs.

Two are brown and three are spotted.

They have pink noses and curly tails.

We named them Spot, Curly, Brownie, Squeakie, and
Punch.

A little girl came to see our pigs. Her name is Lou.

The mother pig watched her babies to see that we did not
hurt them.

I watched the mother pig. You cannot see her in the
picture, but she is not far away.

THE COLTS

These are Uncle Tom's mule colts.
He lets me feed them.
I give them corn and clover.
Sometimes I give them salt and sugar.
They like salt and sugar. It makes them tame.
The colts like to play. They run, jump, and kick.
They kick each other, but they do not kick me.
Big Boy and Little Boy like to feed the mule colts, too.

MOTHER'S COW

Mother has a gentle cow. I can lead her.
She likes me to find green grass for her to eat.
I can milk the cow.
The milk is good for me.
It makes me grow right.
Sometimes Mother makes ice cream from the milk.
She lets us ask our friends to come and have a party.

KIT AND MARY

Kit and Mary are Daddy's big mules.
Sometimes Daddy lets us ride Kit.
Mary does not like to have little boys ride her.
One day Alton and I rode down by the woods.
A calf jumped out of the woods.
Kit jumped out of the road.
Guess what happened to Alton and me!

GRANDMOTHER'S CALF

This is Grandmother's calf.
She lets us play with him.
He knows how to play with little boys.
When we run and jump, he runs and jumps, too.
Sometimes he lies down when we lie down.
At night he sleeps in the barn.
We made him a nice bed of straw.
He rubs his head against us to show that he is glad.

[38]

BOSS, A DOG PLAYMATE

Boss is Uncle Tom's big dog.

If he does not know you, he barks and barks.

He does not bark at me. He wags his tail.

Then I know he is glad to see me.

We like to have Boss come to play with us.

If there are snakes, he finds them and kills them.

He does not like to leave us.

We have to lead him home with a chain.

Then I say, "Good-by, Boss. Come and play with us again
some day."

WADING

We have a little brook on our farm.
We built a dam in it.
Now we have a nice pond.
We can wade in the pond.
We make little boats and sail them on the water.
A big leaf makes a good sail.
Little fish live in the brook.
It is fun to catch them.
They are too small to eat.
We put them back into the water.
We do not hurt them.
It is fun to play in the cool water.

OUR CART

Daddy has a cart. He made it himself.
Sometimes he lets us play with it.
One day the little twins said, "We want to ride in the cart."
So Raeford said, "Get in. We will give you a ride."
I got in, too, and away we went.
Raeford and Big Boy pulled us.
Then Raeford and Big Boy pulled the cart down hill.
Faster and faster it went.
Raeford and Big Boy had to run to keep ahead of it.

"Look out!" cried Raeford.

"We are going to stop if we can."

I thought, "Maybe they can't stop!"

We sat down in the bottom of the cart.

Raeford and Big Boy turned the cart off the road.

When they let go of the front, we slid out of the back.

It did not hurt us. We picked ourselves up and laughed
   and laughed.

Then we had to get the cart up the hill again.

TAKING OUR GOAT TO RIDE

One day our cousin John Henry came to play with us.

We did not know what to play.

I said, "Let's take our goat to ride."

We put Nannie in the cart, and John Henry held the chain
so that she would not jump out.

But she did not try to jump out. She liked to ride.

At last we were all tired. But Nannie was not tired.

When we took off her chain, she jumped out of the cart,
and over Rufus' head!

HARVESTING WHEAT

Daddy said, "The wheat is yellow. It is ripe.
Mr. Pender wants us to help him cut his wheat."
Daddy drove the tractor.
The reaper cut the wheat and tied it in bundles.
We picked up the bundles and put them in piles.
Then a man went to the piles and made them into shocks.
We like to help harvest the wheat.

GATHERING WILD GRAPES

One day the little twins and I went fishing, but the fish
would not bite.

I said, "Let's set our hooks and look for wild grapes."

So we set our hooks and began to look.

Soon we found a big grape vine. It was high up in a tree.

The little twins climbed the tree and began eating grapes.

I went to look for another grape vine.

I heard something and looked up.

There was a big black snake right over my head.

It was looking down at me!

The little twins saw me run. They came down the tree fast.

I said, "I saw a big black snake."

We all ran home as fast as we could go.

"Where are your fish?" said Mother.

"We forgot to look at our hooks," I said. "We set our
hooks and went to look for wild grapes. A big black
snake was in the tree. We ran!"

"A black snake will not hurt you," said Mother.

I said, "A snake is a snake!"

Mother laughed. Then she said, "When you get older,
you will know better." I wonder!

IN THE TOBACCO FIELD

One night at supper Daddy said, "We must all go to bed
   early. Tomorrow we have some hard work to do."
In the morning we went to the tobacco field with Daddy.
The tobacco plants were taller than little Rufus.
The bottom leaves were yellow.
All day we helped Daddy pick the bottom leaves.
We put the leaves in the sled.
When the sled was full, Kit pulled it to the tobacco barn.
Then we filled the sled again.
We did this over and over.
Mother and our big sisters worked at the tobacco barn.
They put the leaves in bunches with the stems together.
Then they tied the bunches of leaves to long sticks, and
   hung them in the tobacco barn.
The next day more leaves were yellow, and we helped
   Daddy pick them again.
When the tobacco barn was full, Daddy built fires to
   "cure" the tobacco.
He watched the fires day and night, so that the tobacco
   would not get too hot.
We are too little to watch the fires.
When we get big like Daddy we can do that, too.

HARVESTING SWEET POTATOES

"Boys," said Daddy, "we can dig the sweet potatoes today.
I want you to help me."
Daddy dug the potatoes.
We picked them up and put them in baskets and buckets.
Then Daddy put them in the wagon and pulled them to the
house.
"We have enough to last all winter," said Daddy.
I was glad. I like sweet potatoes.

RIDING IN A TIRE

Big Boy, Little Boy, and I are too big to ride in a tire.
William says that it makes him dizzy, but Rufus likes
   to ride in a tire.
He gets in the tire and we roll it in a smooth place.
If we go over bumps, it hurts his head.
Rufus says, "Everything stands on its head when I ride in
   a tire!"
I wish I could ride in a tire.   I want to see trees and houses
   standing on their heads.

PICKING COTTON

"Boys, get your bags. The cotton is ready to pick," said Daddy.

We got our bags and went to the field.

We picked and picked.

I began to get hungry.

My arms began to hurt. Would lunch time never come?

Then Mother called, "Lunch is ready."

The cabbage and potatoes were good.

The sweet potato pie was good, too.

I said, "Mother, why does Daddy plant cotton? I do not like to pick it. It makes my arms hurt."

Mother said, "Daddy plants cotton to buy clothes for you to wear to school."

"But who buys the cotton?" I asked. "What do they do with it?"

"It is sold to the factory," said Mother. "They spin it into thread. They make cloth for your shirts and your overalls."

"I did not know that," I said. "I will pick the cotton."

AT THE COTTON GIN

One day we went with Daddy to the cotton gin.
The cotton gin takes the seed out of the cotton.
Then the cotton is made into big bales.
Raeford and I climbed up to look at the bales.
Raeford said, "Let's play that we are going to buy the
    cotton and take it to the factory."
So we played that we were men buying cotton.
One cotton bale was cut to show the cotton.
I looked at it the way the men do.
I said, "This is very good cotton."

MAKING MOLASSES

Every year Daddy plants some sugar cane.
He says that all little boys like molasses.
We help Daddy hoe the cane.
The cane grows very tall, like corn.
We help him tear the leaves off.
We help him cut it down and take it to the mill.

AT THE MILL

First we put the sugar cane in the mill.
Kit turns the mill and the juice comes out.
Then the juice is boiled and boiled.
Soon it is thick and good.
Sometimes we take little pans to the mill.
We cook some juice until it is very thick.
Then we pull it and make candy.
Other boys and girls come to help us.
We all have a good time.

HALLOWE'EN FUN

Mr. Narvie lives in a little old house on the hill.

He lives all alone.

On Hallowe'en night we made some jack-o'-lanterns.

Big Boy said, "Mr. Narvie is not at home. He will not get back until after dark. Let's play ghosts and scare him when he comes home."

Little Boy said, "I will carry the black cat."

I said, "I will carry the jack-o'-lantern."

We put the jack-o'-lantern near Mr. Narvie's door.

Then we stood very still in the dark.

Soon we heard Mr. Narvie coming. He was singing.

He did not see the jack-o'-lantern at first.

Then the black cat mewed. Mr. Narvie stopped and turned around.

We thought he was going to run, but he did not.

He laughed and said, "Come, boys. I know it's you!"

We went in. He gave us apples, candy, and peanuts.

Mr. Narvie always has good things to eat.

MAKING A RABBIT TRAP

One morning there was a big white frost.
Daddy said, "There is a frost this morning. Let's catch a
  rabbit. Mother will bake it for us."
All the twins cried, "Oh, yes! Let's catch a rabbit!"
Raeford said, "We will make a trap first."
We got some boards and nails.
Soon we had a good rabbit trap.
Then we found a rabbit's path.
It was under a persimmon tree.
We set the trap in the path.
Next morning I went to the trap.
The door was shut.
I called, "The door is shut!"
Raeford came. Rufus came. The big twins came.

We looked under the door of the trap.

It was not a rabbit.

What could it be?

Little Boy pulled it out.

"Possum and sweet potatoes!" cried Little Boy.

"Possum and sweet potatoes!" cried all the children.

We all like possum and sweet potatoes.

Mother bakes it for us.

But first we had to put the possum in a cage, and feed him
   to make him fat.

THE POSSUM

Possums have long strong tails.

They can hang by their tails from trees.

They have sharp teeth and claws, too.

You have to carry them by their tails or on a stick so
that they will not bite you.

We put our possum on a stick and I carried him home.

We did not have a good cage.

So we put him in an old chicken coop.

We fed him persimmons.

The next morning we went to feed him.

The coop was empty!

The possum had gone back to his home.

The old coop did not hold him.

We said, "No possum and sweet potatoes this time!"

HELPING DADDY

Daddy said, "It is cold tonight.   We shall need much wood."
I said, "Daddy, you are tired.   We will get the wood."
Big Boy and Little Boy sawed the wood.
I carried it to the house.
We like to get the wood for Daddy.
We like to help him when he is tired.

THANKSGIVING

"Tomorrow is Thanksgiving," said Mother. "What shall
we have for dinner?"

"I will get some pears and apples," said Raeford.

The big twins said, "We will go to the field and get some
peanuts."

"We will find some hickory nuts," said the little twins.

I said, "I will go to Daddy's cornfield and find a
pumpkin."

"Good," said Mother. "I will bake some chickens. Your
sisters may bake some cakes and sweet potato pies."

Just then Daddy came with some rabbits.

Everybody did something for our dinner.

When it was ready, there were so many things on the
table that we could hardly see the table cloth.

Uncle Tom came to have dinner with us.

He told us funny stories and made us laugh.

We had a fine time.

I wish that Thanksgiving came every day.

PEANUTS

Daddy planted a big patch of peanuts.

We hoed them many times.

They grew and grew.

We could not see the peanuts.

They grow in the ground.

At last Daddy said, "The peanuts are ready to harvest."

Then he plowed them up.

We picked them off the vines and carried them home.

In winter we sit by the fire and roast and eat peanuts.

Sometimes Mother and Daddy tell us stories and sing
   until we can't keep our eyes open.

When we are full of peanuts and stories, we go to bed.

SANTA CLAUS

It was almost Christmas.

The twins and I had never seen Santa Claus.

I said, "Mother, we want to see Santa Claus. May we
stay up on Christmas-eve night and see him?"

Mother smiled, but she did not say anything.

We went back to the yard to play.

Big Boy said, "Let's be good and do everything Mother
wants us to do. Then we will ask her again."

We cleaned the yard, we carried in wood, we milked the
cows, we fed the pigs.

The night before Christmas Little Boy said, "Please,
Mother, let us stay up tonight and see Santa Claus!"

Then Mother smiled and said "Yes."

We sat by the fire and waited. The little twins went to
sleep.

At last we heard an automobile. Mother went to the door.

Someone said, "Tell your boys to come and get their bags."

We went to the automobile, and there was Santa Claus!

He had a long white beard, and he wore a red coat.

Santa Claus said, "Here are your bags, boys."

We said "Thank you! Thank you, Santa Claus!"

Then away he went!

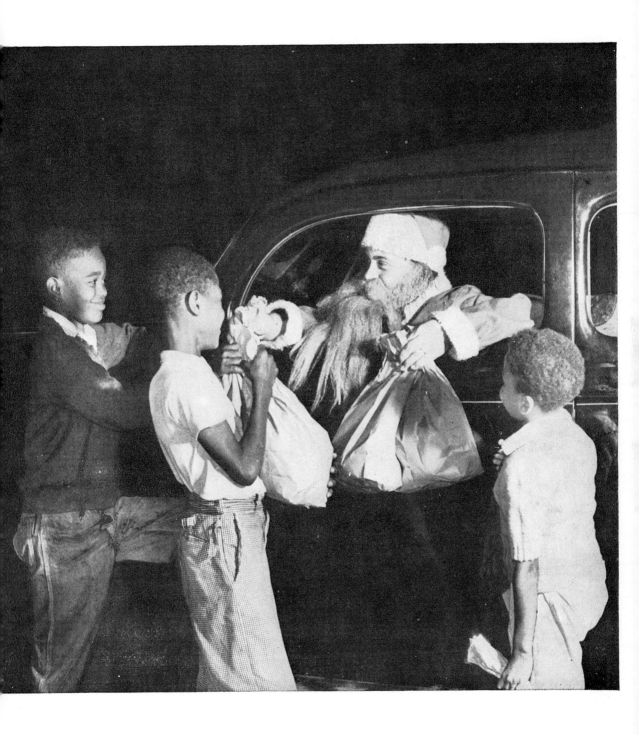

We took our bags into the house.

The card said, "A Merry Christmas from Santa Claus."

I said, "Mother, I thought he would drive a sleigh."

"Next year he may come in an airplane!" said Mother.

Then she put the bags away for our Christmas tree, and
we went to bed.

Early Christmas morning we saw the Christmas tree.

It was the best we ever had.

We found candy and nuts and oranges and toys.

But the best thing was that we had seen Santa Claus.

TURNING THE GRINDSTONE

One night Daddy said, "My ax is getting dull. We will grind it tomorrow."

The big twins and I do not like to turn the grindstone.

The little twins are too little to turn it.

Next morning at breakfast I said, "I do not want any cereal." I ate a piece of toast. Then I said, "Mother, please excuse me."

Big Boy saw me, and he thought of the grindstone. He ate his cereal and said, "I do not want any toast." Then he asked Mother to excuse him.

We ran to the woods.

Then Little Boy thought of the grindstone. He had many things on his plate, but he asked Mother to excuse him.

She said, "You must eat your breakfast first."

Daddy said, "I want you to turn the grindstone."

So Little Boy had to turn the grindstone.

Then Big Boy and I went back to the house.

Little Boy would not talk to us.

Big Boy said, "Little Boy, did you like your breakfast?"

Then he ran so fast that Little Boy could not catch him.

THE TIN BOX

One day I went to the mail box for Mother.

Our mail box is down by the road.

A big boy was working in the field near the box.

He pulled my hair and ears. He tore my shirt.

I ran home as fast as I could.

Another day I went to the mail box.

The big boy was there.

He pulled my hair and ears. He tore my shirt.

I pulled away from him and ran home.

I said to Mother, "I do not want to go to the mail box again.
  A big boy was there. He pulled my hair and ears. He
  tore my shirt."

One morning Mother gave me a tin box.

She said, "Here is a nice tin box. There is pepper in it.
  You will know what to do with it. I want you to go to
  the mail box for me."

I put the tin box in my pocket.

Then I went to the mail box.

The big boy was there.

He came near me.

Then I took the lid off my tin box.

I said, "Please don't make me throw this pepper. It is
not good for the eyes."

He put his hands over his eyes.

Then he ran as fast as he could.

He ran and ran.

I do not know how far he went, but he never came back.

[89]

MY GARDEN

When Spring came, Daddy planted a big garden.
We helped him plant it.
We planted onions, peas, turnips, and many other things.
Then I said, "Daddy, I want a garden. Where can I plant
　it?"
"You may plant it where I had potatoes last year," said
　Daddy.
I dug the ground.
I raked it and made it fine.
Then I planted sweet potatoes, beans, and corn.
I hoed it many times.
My potatoes and beans grew, but my corn did not grow
　right.
I went to Daddy.
I said, "My corn did not grow right. It did not grow tall."
Daddy said, "You planted it too thick. Next time plant it
　farther apart and it will grow tall."
Next year I will grow my corn right.

THE FLOWER GARDEN

My sisters like flowers.

They planted a big flower garden.

They hoed and hoed the plants, and watered them every day.

Now they have many pretty flowers.

Sometimes I help my sisters take care of their garden.

They give me flowers to take to my teacher.

THE TERRAPIN

I like to watch this little terrapin.
His shell is pretty, but his face is not.
We found him by the pond.
He cannot go fast.   He walks all the time.
He does not have to run to get out of the rain.
He carries his house with him, everywhere he goes.
He can pull his head and feet into his house.
Aunt Susan said, "If a terrapin bites you, he will not let
   go till it thunders."
We do not know when it will thunder.
So we do not touch the terrapin.

[96]

THE LITTLE BULLFROG

Rufus caught this little bullfrog near the pond.

First the bullfrog was a tadpole.

Then he was a little frog.

He is not very big now, but his legs are long.

His back is green, and it shines in the sun.

Rufus is not afraid to hold the little bullfrog.

If frogs bite, they do not hold on till it thunders, as
terrapins do.

Rufus will not hurt the little frog.

Soon he will put him back in the pond.

We like to see frogs jump.

When they are scared, they can jump farther than we can.

We like best of all to hear the frogs sing.

All the frogs in the pond sing when spring comes.

[98]

MY WHISTLES

One day Mother said, "Tobe, please go to the garden and get some beans and tomatoes for dinner."

I started to the garden.

I heard Little Boy say, "Come on, boys, we will be gone when he gets back."

I did not look back or say anything.

I knew that they would go to the pond in the woods.

I picked the beans and tomatoes.

Then I cut some stems from the pumpkin leaves and put them in my pocket.

I carried the beans and tomatoes to Mother.

Then I ran to the pond.

Sure enough, the big twins and Raeford were wading in the water. They did not see me. I hid in the bushes.

I made whistles from the stems of the pumpkin leaves.

I made one big whistle and one little whistle.

First I blew the little whistle. They stood very still and listened.

Then I blew the big whistle. They jumped out of the pond and ran home as fast as they could.

Now the big twins will not go with me to the pond, but they will not tell me why.

I DID NOT GET A NICKEL

One day I wanted a nickel.

I went to Aunt Mary's and said, "May I work for you today?"

Aunt Mary said, "Yes, you may go to Mr. Pender's for me."

I started to Mr. Pender's.

I saw a snake's track in the road.

I was scared, but I kept on going.

Soon I saw a big snake in the road.

I ran back to Aunt Mary's.

I said, "I did not go to Mr. Pender's.

I saw a big snake in the road."

Aunt Mary said, "Why didn't you go around the snake?"

I had not thought of that.

I did not get the nickel.

IN THE STRAWBERRY PATCH

One day Mother said, "I want some strawberries for
   dinner. Who will get them for me?"

"We will," said the little twins.

They got big buckets and went to the strawberry patch.

They stayed and stayed.

Then Mother said, "Who will go and look for William
   and Rufus?"

"I will," said Big Boy.

Soon he found the little twins.

They were sitting by their buckets in the strawberry
   patch.

"Why did you stay so long?" asked Big Boy.

"We could not carry our buckets," they said.

Sure enough, they could not, for they had picked the big
   buckets full.

The little twins were hot and tired, but they had put
   leaves on top of the buckets to keep the strawberries
   cool.

FINDING A BEE TREE

One day I went fishing.

Big Boy and the little twins went with me.

We fished and fished, but the fish did not bite.

Then we saw some little bees near the brook.

"There must be a bee tree near here," said Big Boy.

I said, "Let's find it."

We set our hooks and began to look for the bee tree.

[106]

We looked at all the trees on one hill.
Then we looked at all the trees on another hill.
"I give up," said Big Boy.
"I don't," I said. "Listen, I hear bees now."
Sure enough, there they were.
"They are coming out of that big oak tree," I said.
We ran home and told Daddy.
Daddy said, "We will get them tonight."
We did, too.
We got pounds and pounds of honey.
It is fun to find a bee tree.

MAKING ICE CREAM

"It is hot today," said Mother. "Shall I make some ice cream?"

We said, "Oh, yes, Mother. Please make some ice cream!"

Mother said, "Can you find some ripe strawberries?"

I said, "Yes, who will help me?"

"We will," said Big Boy and the little twins.

We found many ripe strawberries.

Mother got some ice.

Then she mixed milk and sugar and strawberries and put them in the ice cream freezer.

Raeford turned the freezer.

We could hardly wait.

Soon we had four quarts of strawberry ice cream.

PICKING BLACKBERRIES

Many blackberries grow on our farm.

When they are ripe, we pick some every day.

Mother puts them in cans for winter.

Rufus gets more berries than William does.

One day Mother said, "William, why do you let Rufus
pick more berries than you do?"

"He does not," said William. "He eats one and puts
three in his bucket. I eat two and put two in my
bucket."

TOMATOES FOR WINTER

One day Mother said, "Boys, I want you to pick some tomatoes for me to can. We shall need many cans of tomatoes this winter."

We picked tomatoes and tomatoes and tomatoes.

Then we put them in Daddy's cart and pulled them to the house.

I asked, "How many quarts will these make?"

Mother said, "If all the tomatoes are good, they will make about sixty quarts."

"Will that be enough for winter?" I asked.

Mother said, "No, we shall need two hundred quarts of tomatoes."

"Whoop-ee!" said Little Boy. "How many cans of food do we eat in the winter?"

Mother said, "We ate six hundred quarts last year."

"Well," said Little Boy, "I never felt as if I had too much. We'll pick more tomatoes!"

PICKING PEACHES

One morning Uncle Tom called, "Come, boys, help me
pick my peaches. Put the large smooth ones in the
basket. You may have the others."
We picked peaches all day. We put the large smooth
ones in the baskets. We kept all the others.
We ate peaches all that day.
We ate peaches all the next day.
Yet we wanted more.

[116]

BIG BOY'S POCKETS

"Big Boy, what do you have in your pockets?" said Mother.
"Oh, just a few things," said Big Boy.
"Please put them on the table," said Mother. "I want
to see them."
This is what Big Boy put on the table:

Two big pears	One clean handkerchief
Four little apples	Two soiled handkerchiefs
Three sweet potatoes	A fish hook
A tin box full of sugar	A rabbit's foot
A ball	Yards and yards of string.

The rabbit's foot was for good luck.
Mother said, "There's no such thing as luck."
So Big Boy gave Mother his rabbit's foot.

OUR MERRY-GO-ROUND

Rufus and William wanted a merry-go-round.
Big Boy and Little Boy made one for them.
They did not make it like the one at the fair.
First they sawed a post from a little tree.
They planted one end of the post in the ground.
They bored a big hole in the top of the post.
In the hole they put a short iron rod.
They took a long board and made a round hole in the
middle of it.
Then they put the board on the post, so that the iron rod
came up through the hole in the board.
When they pushed the board, it went round and round
on the iron rod.
William got on one end of the board.
Rufus got on the other end of the board.
They made it go round and round.
"Everything is black!" said William, and off he fell.
Next time they did not ride so fast.
We all had fun on the merry-go-round.

[119]

WHAT BRINGS GOOD LUCK?

One day last summer we went to see Aunt Susan.
Her apple trees were full of apples.
I said, "I am glad you have many apples. We do not have
many apples on our trees."
She asked, "Did you hang horse-shoes in your apple trees?"
"No, we did not do that," I said.
"You should hang horse-shoes in your apple trees
if you want many apples," she said.
We went home and told Mother.
She said, "The horse-shoes did not make the apples grow.
Work made them grow. You will have to dig around
our trees and spray them."
We did, too.
Now we have many apples.